THE SHADE
OF DEATH

KrabB
MASTER OF THE SEA

With special thanks to Michael Ford

For William Nettleton, strong and kind

www.beastquest.co.uk

ORCHARD BOOKS
338 Euston Road, London NW1 3BH
Orchard Books Australia
Level 17/207 Kent St, Sydney, NSW 2000

A Paperback Original
First published in Great Britain in 2009

Beast Quest is a registered trademark of Working Partners Limited
Series created by Working Partners Limited, London

Text © Working Partners Limited 2009
Cover and inside illustrations by Steve Sims © Orchard Books 2009

A CIP catalogue record for this book is available from
the British Library.

ISBN 978 1 40830 437 2

9 10 8

Printed in the UK by CPI Bookmarque, Croydon, CR0 4TD

The paper and board used in this paperback are natural recyclable
products made from wood grown in sustainable forests. The
manufacturing processes conform to the environmental regulations of
the country of origin.

Orchard Books is a division of Hachette Children's Books,
an Hachette UK company

www.hachette.co.uk

KrabB
MASTER OF THE SEA

BY ADAM BLADE

ORCHARD BOOKS

Welcome to a new world...

Did you think you'd seen all the evil that existed? You're almost as foolish as Tom! He may have conquered Wizard Malvel, but fresh challenges await him. He must travel far and leave behind everything he knows and loves. Why? Because he has six Beasts to defeat in a kingdom he can't even call home.

Will his heart be in it? Or will Tom turn his back on this latest Quest? Little does he know, but he has close ties to the people here. And a new enemy determined to ruin him. Can you guess who that enemy is...?

Read on to see how your hero fares.

Velmal

PROLOGUE

Castor loved the feel of sand between
his toes, but he had work to do. The
fish wouldn't just jump into his net.

He pushed his small fishing boat
into the shallows and rowed out
to sea. He was grateful for the sun
warming his face – it was only on
days like these, warm and calm,
that his father let him go out fishing
alone. He headed for deeper water,
where he knew large shoals of fish

liked to gather. It wasn't long before he saw the telltale signs a few boat-lengths away – a dark patch of water where the fish were feeding near the surface.

Spreading his feet to keep his balance, Castor stood up and tossed his weighted net into the water. He kept hold of the ropes attached to either side of the net and watched the mesh land right over the shoal of fish. A perfect throw!

Bracing his foot against the edge of the little boat, he pulled the net back. It was heavy – a great catch, more than enough for one day's work! With any luck, he'd be at the market before breakfast, and home in time for lunch. He felt his heart race happily. His father was the finest fisherman in all of Gwildor, and Castor was sure to make him proud today.

As he hauled the fish-filled net on board, something caught his eye. A dark shape in the distant east, floating on the water.

"A boat from Avantia?" he wondered aloud.

Castor felt the net slip from his hands, and immediately saw his precious catch spilling back into the water. He scrambled to save it, but only managed to retrieve half of the fish. The rest escaped back into the sea.

Fool! he cursed himself.

When he looked up again, the other boat had sailed out of sight.

Something broke the water just ahead of him, black and narrow like the beam of a sunken vessel floating back to the surface. As Castor squinted at it, a huge wave burst upwards, drenching him to the skin. Blinded by the seawater, he turned away, spluttering.

When his eyes cleared, he froze with fear. Eight long, spindly legs arced above the waves, tendrils of slime and seaweed hanging from them. Castor forgot all about his catch and stumbled backwards, his eyes fixed in horror upon the creature emerging from the sea.

Its body was much bigger than Castor's boat and barnacles clung like warts to its belly. Two evil eyes glittered above the wide gash of a mouth. It was a giant crab!

The creature stood on the water, stabbing the waves with its legs, then scuttled across the surface as though it were walking on solid ground. Two giant pincers gnashed at the air, making dreadful snapping sounds.

Castor grabbed his oars and began frantically rowing towards the shore. But the creature was moving too quickly. It was above him in a heartbeat, blocking out the sun with its bulk.

Now that the giant crab was up close, Castor could see that one of its pincers dripped with green venom. In a flash, the Beast slashed at the boat and Castor ducked his head. There was a cracking sound and the boat shook. When Castor looked again he saw that half of his vessel – and all of his catch – had gone. Water rushed into the remaining half of the boat and the sea poured in around his ankles. He was sinking!

Castor clung onto his broken boat as the Beast turned to face him. In its eyes Castor saw only hate. "What are you?" he yelled at the creature.

The Beast made a sound like a screeching seabird, and the pincer that dripped with venom darted forwards. Castor turned to leap away from the wrecked boat, but a sharp pain shot up through his back. He fell down. His vision blurred, and his limbs felt suddenly heavy.

Castor tried to reach for one of the oars, but he had no strength left. His eyes began to droop as he stared at the distant shore of Gwildor. He would not be taking home the catch that would make his father proud. He doubted that he was even going to make it home alive...

CHAPTER ONE

A NEW QUEST

"Are you *sure* you know where you're going?" Tom asked Aduro.

"It's around here somewhere," replied the good wizard, striding ahead and rapping his knuckles on the next door along the passageway.

Tom laughed and looked at Elenna. She grinned at him.

They were following Aduro along the maze-like corridors beneath King Hugo's palace.

A shape loomed out of the darkness and Tom's hand reached for his sword, ready to face an intruder. But as the glow of Aduro's flaming torch illuminated the passage, he saw that the figure was simply a suit of armour. The helmet and breastplate gleamed, reminding Tom of the magical golden armour he had rescued on a previous Beast Quest.

"I had no idea these tunnels even existed," said Elenna.

"The palace holds many secrets," said Aduro. "I doubt even the King himself knows them all."

The wizard came to a sudden stop in the middle of the passageway, almost causing Tom and Elenna to bump into him. Tom saw that Aduro was running his fingers across the wall. "Here we are!"

Tom looked at the wall in confusion. There was no sign of a door – just bare stone with patches of green moss.

"Where *are* we?" asked Tom.

Aduro lifted his staff and moved the tip in a circle over the wall. Tom heard Elenna gasp as a crack appeared in the stone surface, creaking open to form a doorway.

"This way," said Aduro.

Tom and his friend followed the wizard into a gloomy chamber. He couldn't see more than a few paces ahead of him, but Aduro struck his staff firmly on the ground, and suddenly the room blazed as if lit by thousands of candles.

Now Tom could see a huge steaming cauldron in the middle of the room. Around the walls, on many tiers of shelves, hundreds of glass vials held liquids and powders of many different colours. *This must be the place where Aduro does his most powerful magic*, Tom thought.

He heard a noise and turned. Standing just inside the door was a figure he recognised. "Father! Where did you come from?" Tom cried, as happiness flooded through him.

Taladon smiled. "I was behind you the whole time."

"But how?" asked Elenna. "We didn't hear you."

"Once you've tracked as many Beasts as I have, you'll be able to move just as silently," Taladon replied.

Tom felt a grin break out over his face. Until a few days ago, he'd thought Taladon was dead – he could still hardly believe his father was here in the flesh.

"Maybe you can teach me your technique," Tom said. "We can go out tomorrow and practise. Wait till you see Storm – he's the fastest stallion in Avantia…" Tom trailed off when he saw the anxious look in his father's eyes. "What is it?" he asked. He knew that something important was on Taladon's mind.

"I think," began Taladon, looking over Tom's shoulder at Aduro, "our fun will have to wait a while longer."

Across the room, Aduro cleared his throat and Tom turned to look at him. He was holding something in his palm, and Tom took a few paces towards the wizard. He recognised the object as the amulet he'd pieced together on his previous Quest to the Forbidden Land. Taladon had been a ghost until the fragments had been put back together.

"Watch," said Aduro, dangling the amulet in front of him.

It glowed as bright as a star in the wizard's hand. Beams of white light flashed out from its centre. Then it twirled round to reveal the map that was on its reverse. Tom watched, astonished, as mountains grew up from the amulet, and clusters of buildings appeared to mark settlements and towns. Trees glowed green where forests could be found.

"That isn't Avantia," Tom murmured.

"The amulet will show its owner the way through *any* land," said Taladon. "You must trust it always."

"And where is that place?" asked Tom, peering closely at the fringes of the map, where a clear blue sea lapped at a sandy shore.

Aduro dropped the amulet into Tom's hand and the light faded. "That was the land of Gwildor," said the wizard, gazing at Tom. "Where your next Beast Quest awaits…"

CHAPTER TWO

BEYOND THE WESTERN OCEAN

"I've never heard of Gwildor,"
said Elenna.

Tom nodded in agreement as he
clutched the amulet in his hand.

"Everything has its twin," Aduro
said. "A companion and an opposite.
It keeps the universe in balance."

"Gwildor is Avantia's twin
kingdom?" Tom asked.

"Yes," said Aduro. "For many years, the people of Gwildor lived in peace. But now evil has taken hold of Gwildor. Beasts are wreaking havoc and destroying people's lives."

Tom looked at Taladon sadly. He'd been looking forward to spending more time with his father, but he knew now that it would have to wait a while longer.

Taladon placed a hand on Tom's shoulder. "There'll be other times, my son," he said. "Right now, Gwildor needs you."

"But doesn't Gwildor have its own Master of the Beasts?" asked Elenna.

Tom saw Aduro and Taladon share a look. Something was worrying them.

"Gwildor once had its own champion – a *Mistress* of the Beasts, to be precise – but she…changed."

A look of pain wrinkled Aduro's brow. "I can say no more. We must prepare."

"That's if you accept the challenge, Tom," said Taladon. "After all, you've faced more than your fair share of Beasts for one so young. If you feel the need to rest a while in the castle…"

"No," said Tom, standing straighter. "If we allow evil to flourish in Gwildor, Avantia could be next to suffer."

Taladon smiled. "I wish I could join you on this Quest, but I must stay here and become Master of the Beasts once again."

"Don't worry, he'll have me to look out for him," Elenna said, stepping forwards. "But where is Gwildor?"

"Across the Western Ocean," said Aduro. "A day's travel by boat."

"The journey can be dangerous," said Taladon. "Storms descend in the blink of an eye."

"We'll make it," said Tom. "And when we do, no Beast will be safe."

Taladon lifted a hand. "No, Tom, the Beasts of Gwildor are not evil. They are bewitched by dark magic. You must *free* them, not destroy them."

Tom nodded. He'd seen good Beasts enchanted with dark magic before. On his first ever Quest he had freed the good Beasts of Avantia from an evil spell cast by Wizard Malvel. "I don't understand," he said. "I'd hoped we'd seen the last of Malvel and his magic."

Aduro shook his head. "Malvel is not your enemy. He is still recovering from your most recent battle, somewhere in the wilds of Gorgonia."

"Then who has taken control of Gwildor's Beasts?" asked Elenna.

"His name is Velmal," said Aduro. "Just as Gwildor is the twin of Avantia, so too does it have its own Dark Wizard."

"Velmal?" said Tom. "You've never mentioned him before."

Aduro sighed. "Until recently there was no need. Velmal has been imprisoned for many years in a Gwildorian dungeon. But he has escaped…"

"How do you know all this?" asked Elenna.

"My magic is not as strong in Gwildor as it is in Avantia," said Aduro, "but I feel enough to sense when danger approaches."

Tom felt anger boil within him. He

swore to himself that he'd defeat Velmal and save Gwildor's good Beasts. "What Beasts will we have to free?" he asked.

"There isn't time to explain," answered Taladon. "Just know that they are more ferocious than anything Avantia holds. And perhaps they are even stronger now. I have not faced the Gwildorian Beasts for many years. Not since..." He paused. "Since I imprisoned Velmal."

"You must make haste," said Aduro, walking to the cauldron. In his hand he held a vial of purple liquid. "I will send you to the western shore of Avantia – where a boat will be waiting for you."

Taladon put his hand firmly on Tom's shoulder again. "Farewell, Tom," he said.

Aduro carefully tipped the vial and a single drop of liquid fell into the cauldron. A cloud of purple smoke spread all around them. Tom suddenly felt his feet leave the ground. He saw Elenna rise, too. Taladon and Aduro began to shrink below them as Tom and his friend were lifted into the air.

"Goodbye, Father," Tom shouted. He saw Taladon wave solemnly, before the room disappeared completely.

CHAPTER THREE

A NEW KINGDOM, A NEW BEAST

Tom suddenly smelt salt on the air, and as he felt himself being lowered down his feet sank into something soft. Sand!

"The western shore!" said Elenna.

Tom turned to look about him in disbelief. Elenna was right – they'd been here before to rescue Sepron the sea serpent.

"I never knew Aduro's magic was *this* powerful!" said Tom.

In one direction, golden sand stretched out as far as he could see. In the other, a rocky headland jutted out into the ocean. In the blustery wind, the ocean's waves were choppy and green. A boat with a sturdy central mast and furled sail lolled at an angle on the sand.

"That must be ours!" said Elenna.

Tom nodded, staring out to sea. Over the water – somewhere – Gwildor awaited. As he took it all in, he realised what was missing.

"Storm and Silver!" he said. He and Elenna had been accompanied by their faithful animal friends on every Quest so far. The thought of travelling without them was daunting.

Suddenly, the air beside the boat began to shimmer. Two shapes formed, one larger than the other. Tom made out Storm's muscular body, then Silver's lithe form. As the haze vanished, the stallion and the wolf were left standing on the beach. Storm shook his mane and cantered towards them, his hooves churning up the sand.

"I'm so glad they're here!" said Elenna.

Silver began running in a wide circle, sniffing and snapping at the waves. Tom checked Storm's bulging saddlebags. Inside, there was bread, cheese and dried meat. Their water flasks were also full. His trusty shield hung from the saddle – he'd lost count of the number of times it had saved his life.

"Come on," he said to Elenna, putting the shield on his arm. "There's no time to waste."

They pushed the boat out into the shallows. The cold water lapped around Tom's ankles as he hopped inside the vessel. Elenna held it steady as Tom guided Storm aboard and then tied his reins to the bench. Silver leapt into the boat and lay near the prow. As Tom unfurled the sail and sat beside the tiller, Elenna jumped on board as well.

"Which way, Tom?"

"We go west," he replied. "And when we get to Gwildor, we must hope the amulet will guide us to the first Beast."

The sail soon caught the wind, and the boat cut through the rough sea.

"Here," Tom said, holding his flask

out to Elenna. "We musn't let ourselves get thirsty – the sun's hot today."

They ate some bread and cheese as the sun arced across the sky. By the time they'd finished, Tom noticed that the water was no longer the muddy green of the Avantian coastline, but a shimmering emerald colour. The sky too had altered. Gone were the heavy bruised clouds of the western coast. Now there were no clouds – just a perfect blue sky.

"At least Gwildor looks nothing like Gorgonia!" Elenna said.

Tom laughed. With its dusty landscape and red skies, Gorgonia was a place he'd rather forget.

"We must be near the shore," said Elenna, pointing out a narrow dark line in the distance.

Worry began to gnaw at Tom's heart. *Everything may look beautiful,* he thought, *but evil lurks in Gwildor.*

While Elenna took control of the tiller, Tom pulled out his magic compass. It would tell him what lay ahead. Centering it in his palm and pointing it towards the coast ahead, he watched the needle swing past *Danger* and settle on *Destiny.* It put his mind at rest, a little…

Thunk!

Tom almost dropped the compass overboard as the boat stopped with a sudden jolt.

"What happened?" said Elenna. "I didn't see any rocks."

Tom scrambled to the front of the vessel and peered over the edge. The wood of the hull was dented, but it had held firm and no water was leaking through. Tom could see right to the sandy bottom of the ocean. "That's strange," he said. "There's nothing there."

The boat drifted for a moment, then stopped again with a hollow thump. This time Tom saw a black boulder poking out above the water, glistening in the sunlight. He was confused. Rocks didn't just float in the middle of the sea.

And then it moved, sinking slowly out of sight.

"What is it?" asked Elenna.

"I don't know," Tom replied. Fear made the hairs on the back of his neck stand up. He heard Storm snort behind him – the stallion sensed danger too.

The boulder-like object appeared again, twenty paces away from the starboard bow. It rose out of the water, trailing seaweed. Looking closer, Tom made out two wicked eyes, swivelling madly in the hollows of a thick shell.

The water around them suddenly became rough and Tom hurriedly dropped the sail, hoping that the boat wouldn't capsize. He heard Silver howling nervously as more rock-like fragments broke the surface of the waves. It took Tom a moment to realise what they were – huge jointed legs protruding from the sea. This was no boulder – it was a Beast with eight legs!

As the creature continued to rise from the water, it swung its huge pincers back and forth. Tom noticed that one of the tips pulsed with a strange, bright green substance.

The monster was so huge it blotted out the sun, throwing their tiny vessel into shadow.

A thunderous voice rumbled across the sky, but the creature's deadly mouth wasn't moving.

"Turn back, Avantian fools," the voice said, "or meet your end in the jaws of Krabb, Beast of Gwildor."

CHAPTER FOUR

VELMAL, CURSE OF GWILDOR

Velmal! thought Tom. "We're not going anywhere!" he shouted at the sky.

Silver scrambled onto his feet and scampered to the front of the boat. With two paws planted on the edge, he howled at the terrifying Beast. Krabb took no notice and scuttled across the water towards them, throwing up seawater as he did so.

Tom gasped as he saw that the Beast could walk on the sea's surface. Krabb's two wide pincers were each as big as a person and lined with serrated edges. They snapped in the air and Tom realised they would cut him in half as easily as his sword would slice a leaf.

Krabb loomed above them, rearing up on his back legs. Tom stared into his wide red mouth, which dripped with slime.

"Get back!" Elenna shouted to Silver. The wolf darted out of the way as one of Krabb's claws grasped the boat's prow. The wood splintered between his pincers with a crunch. Tom staggered back as the mast snapped and seawater poured in around the benches. Storm whinnied in panic. Tom knew that he, Elenna and Silver could swim to safety if the boat sank, but he wasn't sure how far Storm could swim.

Tom drew his sword. "Take us into shore!" he called to Elenna.

"Just keep the Beast back," she replied, grabbing the emergency oars and paddling furiously. With the mast destroyed, it was the only way they'd reach safety.

Krabb swung a pincer at them, and it took all of Tom's strength just to parry the blow with the flat edge of his sword. Tom knew that he mustn't hurt Krabb. Aduro had said these Beasts were good – Velmal was the real enemy.

As the damaged boat limped closer to the shore, Krabb turned on the water, lifted an enormous pincer and smashed it down towards the boat.

Tom dived across the deck to take the blow on his shield. The Beast screeched and drew back his pincer.

Krabb loomed over them. The boat pulled away, with Krabb in close pursuit. Each time the Beast fell behind, his legs worked faster and he gained on them.

Elenna paddled desperately while
Tom kept watch on their deadly
opponent. He searched Krabb's
hideous form, looking for some sign
of the enchantment. If Velmal had
cast a spell, that meant there had
to be some mark of evil on the
Beast's body.

"Take over, Tom," said Elenna, panting. "I can't row for much longer. I'll deal with Krabb."

Tom dropped to his knees and took the oars, plunging them into the water and heaving with all his might. Elenna stood up and placed an arrow in her bow.

"No!" he said, still paddling. "You mustn't kill him."

"I'm just going to slow him down," said Elenna. She let the arrow fly, and it lodged in the joint where one of Krabb's front legs met his shell. The Beast screeched and sank out of sight beneath the waves. Tom sighed with relief – the minor wound would keep Krabb back...for now.

"Well done," he said to Elenna, as he paddled the boat inland. She smiled at him, and soon they were able to pull the boat ashore and help Storm and Silver step out onto the beach. Looking around, Tom could see that the Gwildorian coast had perfect white sand, with a cluster of trees fifty paces inland.

"I thought we'd never make it," said Elenna quietly.

"We wouldn't have, if it wasn't for you," Tom replied.

Storm suddenly gave a whinny of warning. Two figures were making their way towards them from the trees – a man and a woman. But they didn't seem quite…human. Tom felt his skin prickle. He could sense that evil was close by.

"Who are they?" murmured Elenna.

Tom stared at the figures. Their bodies were ghostly and surrounded by a smoky purple cloud. He drew his sword, but the male stranger just laughed.

"Put down your weapon," he ordered coldly. "Your sword is useless against me. I am the great Velmal."

So this is Gwildor's Dark Wizard, Tom thought, hearing Silver growl beside Elenna.

Velmal wore a black tunic and his long hair was a fiery red. Unlike Malvel, his arms and legs were thick with muscle, but the cruel lines of his face reminded Tom of his old enemy.

"What do you want?" Tom shouted.

"He's a brave child, isn't he?" said the woman with a smirk. Her voice was low and husky. She stood as tall as Velmal. Her hair was pitch-black, as were her eyes, but they burned brightly at the same time. She wore silver armour, dented and scored with many gashes. Despite Tom's wariness, he felt something else, too – awe. This woman was his enemy, but he felt that they were strangely alike. It was clear she had seen, and won, many battles.

Velmal nodded. "He may be brave, Freya, but he is a fool to come here." He looked at Tom and Elenna with pure hatred. "Malvel has told me about you two. I look forward to your deaths."

"Enough!" said Tom. "I'm here to stop you, Velmal."

"You'll have to stop the six Beasts first, boy! Be warned." The wizard looked pityingly at the woman beside him. "They proved too much for the last champion."

"She must be the Mistress of the Beasts!" whispered Elenna.

Tom frowned. How could Freya now side with a Dark Wizard? His father would never join forces with Malvel! He charged forwards, thrusting his sword at Velmal. But the blade passed straight through him and Tom went sprawling onto the sand.

Velmal smirked and Freya cackled wildly. Tom watched as their images vanished like smoke in a breeze.

"You'll need to be much quicker than that," said the Dark Wizard's fading voice, "if you want to defeat Krabb."

Freya's laughter disappeared and Tom was left alone on the beach with Elenna and their two animal companions.

"Tom, look!" said Elenna, pointing across the water.

He followed the line of her finger and saw something on the sea's surface, moving towards the shore. *Is that Krabb again?* he wondered.

Tom narrowed his eyes. *No, it's the body of a boy.* His face was turned up towards the sky, and his knees and feet bobbed above the surface.

"Come on," Tom said, running into the water. He heard Elenna splashing through the waves behind him. As they neared the floating body, Tom feared the worst.

Had Krabb already taken an innocent life?

CHAPTER FIVE

IN SEARCH OF THE KEY

They waded out until they were waist deep, and Tom warily watched the water for any sign of Krabb. He saw the floating boy's eyelids flutter.

"He's alive!" Tom said. "Come on, let's get him onto land."

Tom locked his arms under the boy's armpits and Elenna lifted his legs. Once they were back on the

beach, they pulled off the boy's wet
shirt to look for any injuries. There
was nothing on his chest, but when
they turned him over they spotted a
strange raised bruise on his lower
back. It looked like a huge green
insect bite.

Tom took the magical talon from his shield – a gift from his old friend, Epos the flame bird. It could quickly heal injuries like cuts and grazes. He held the talon over the boy's wound, but nothing happened.

"It must be poison," said Elenna. "We know the talon can't cure that. Do you think it was…?"

"Krabb?" Tom finished her question, remembering the green tips of one of the Beast's claws. "No doubt."

As they turned the boy onto his back again, his chest rose and fell steadily and Tom hoped he would soon regain consciousness. Silver sniffed along the boy's body, then looked up at Tom and Elenna and whimpered with concern.

"Did Aduro put any herbs in Storm's saddlebag?" Tom asked Elenna. While she went to look, Tom lifted the boy's eyelids. His pupils were wide and unfocused.

"Nothing," said Elenna, striding back towards him. Suddenly she stopped and pointed at Tom's chest. "The amulet!"

Tom looked down and saw that the amulet, which hung around his neck, was glowing. He took it off and held it in his palm, map-side up. The map magically spread out from the centre. Along one edge, a miniature green sea lapped at the coast. A black, crab-like shape stood above the waves offshore, and the word *KRABB* was spelt out beside it. In the other direction, a red line stretched inland from their location, snaking through the line of trees and into the lush green woodland beyond.

"I think the amulet wants me to follow the red line," said Tom, flipping it back over. He looked at his friend. "But you need to stay here with the boy. When he wakes up, he might not know where he is."

"But it could be dangerous," said Elenna.

"Taladon said we could trust the map," Tom told her. "You stay here with Silver. I'll take Storm and see what lies inland – hopefully there'll be something to help us free Krabb from Velmal's enchantment."

Elenna nodded. "Be careful."

Tom swung up onto Storm's saddle and guided the stallion into the trees. Vines hung from branches and fruits of all colours and sizes grew in

59

clusters among the foliage. Fern leaves ten times as big as Tom sprouted from the forest floor, which was carpeted in dark green, spongy moss.

Tom checked the map again and saw that the red line extended further still into the forest's depths. Something moved behind a tree ahead. Tom tugged at Storm's reins to bring his stallion to a halt. He drew his sword and pulled his shield onto his arm as a misty shape flitted between the trunks.

Tom breathed a sigh of relief as he recognised the form coming towards him. It was Aduro! He frowned as the wizard's outline flickered in and out of sight.

"I must be quick, Tom," Aduro said. "My magic isn't strong this far from Avantia."

"I'm glad you're here. I'm following the map, but I'm not sure where it's trying to lead me," Tom said urgently.

"Trust the amulet always," said Aduro. His image flickered again. "It will lead you to the six prizes that will help you free the Beasts."

Tom had to strain to hear the wizard's voice. "What are these prizes?" he asked.

"They once belonged to the Mistress of the Beasts," said Aduro. "Velmal has scattered them throughout Gwildor. Only with the help of the prizes can you free the Beasts."

"But…"

Aduro vanished before Tom could ask any more questions. He was alone in the forest once more, but with the wizard's guidance he felt much more confident about his Quest. He checked the amulet's map again, and galloped onwards. He didn't want to leave Elenna alone for too long.

Soon the red line came to an end, and Tom climbed off Storm's back. He was standing beside a tree so tall he could barely see the top. It was so thick that half a dozen men wouldn't have been able to circle its trunk with their arms. Could this be where he'd find one of the Mistress's prizes? Tom laid his hand against the bark – it felt just like any other tree.

Storm snorted and pawed the ground at the base of the trunk with his front hooves.

"What is it, boy?" Tom asked.

He went to the spot where his stallion was churning up the earth. Storm tossed his head at the trunk. Tom saw something, and leant close to the tree. There was a glimmer through a split in the bark. "What's this?" he murmured to himself.

Taking his sword, he wedged the point into the narrow crack, and prised it open further. The glimmer became a glow, like silver. Tom gripped the broken bark with his hand and pulled as hard as he could. With a crack, the wood splintered away, and a round object dropped into Tom's hand.

It was one of the most beautiful things he'd ever come across – a shining pearl. He'd seen pearls before – Avantian fishermen sometimes found them – but this was different. It was as big as an apple! As he turned it over in his hand, inspecting its smooth, flawless surface, Tom felt a curious, powerful feeling spread through his chest.

"This must be one of Freya's prizes," he murmured. The amulet had worked – it had led him to a weapon against Velmal's magic.

As he slid the pearl carefully into his pocket, the feeling of power diminished, as though it was the pearl's contact with his skin that created it. He set off as quickly as possible to the beach. He didn't know how the pearl would help to free Krabb, but he felt his confidence growing.

"While there's blood in my veins," he said to Storm, rising up in the saddle as they galloped across the sand, "no Beast will remain Velmal's prisoner."

CHAPTER SIX

LURING A BEAST

It took hardly any time to reach
the beach again. Elenna was with the
boy, who was propped up against a
large piece of driftwood and sipping
from one of their water flasks. Silver
barked excitedly as Storm cantered
over to them. As Tom drew closer, he
saw that the driftwood was wreckage
from a small fishing boat. Tackle was
strewn across the sand, and dead fish

were caught up in the remains of the net.

"You're back!" said Elenna. "This is Castor – he's a fisherman from Gwildor. I've told him we came from the East. Castor, this is Tom, my friend. He helped rescue you."

Tom slid off Storm and knelt beside Castor. The boy was pale. "We thought you had drowned," said Tom. "How are you feeling?"

"I've been better," Castor grimaced, "but fishermen are used to rough seas. My father has come home with bruises bigger than this one." He reached around his back and tenderly touched the green mark. Tom saw it was already a little better than when he had left them.

"What happened to you?" asked Elenna.

Castor frowned. "I can't really remember; it's like a bad dream. One moment I was landing the biggest catch of my life, the next this…this *thing*…" He broke off and shook his head. "No, it couldn't have been…"

Tom looked at Elenna and she mouthed "Krabb" silently. He nodded. In Avantia, people thought that the Beasts were nothing more than myths; perhaps it was the same here in Gwildor.

"Did you find anything, Tom?" asked Elenna. "You were gone a long time."

Tom reached into his pocket and carefully took out the giant pearl. As soon as it was in his fingers again, the surge of power flooded his limbs and chest.

"It's beautiful!" gasped Elenna.

Castor's eyes opened wide with amazement. "Where did you get that?" he asked.

Tom told him about his trip into the forest, though he left out the detail about Aduro.

"The Pearl of Gwildor!" said Castor.

"You know about it?" asked Elenna.

"Only as a myth," replied the boy. "The older fishermen often talk of it. It's supposed to give the bearer the ability to breathe underwater, but

only if it's touching their skin…
Wait!" he cried, looking at Tom.
"You're the one!"

The joy in Castor's eyes took Tom
by surprise. "What do you mean?"
he asked.

Castor pointed at the pearl, and
spoke in a distant voice:

"Magic prizes for the deserving,
He, whose bravery is unswerving,
A son of Gwildor, raised in the East,
Will come to save the kingdom's Beasts."

Tom and Elenna looked at each
other in stunned bewilderment.

"It's an ancient prophecy," Castor
explained. "Everyone in Gwildor
knows it. Children sing rhymes
about a time when great Beasts
helped the people. You came from
the East, and now there are Beasts…"
he trailed off.

Tom was confused. "I was born and raised in Avantia. I'm not a son of Gwildor. But listen, what did you say about Beasts?"

Castor looked suddenly shy. "It's nothing. I must still be dazed."

Elenna knelt down at Castor's side and put a comforting hand on his arm. "Tell us. We promise we'll believe you."

Castor looked at them uncertainly. "I was attacked by something. I can barely describe it – a giant crab. That's why I was floating in the water. The Beast ate my catch, and then destroyed my boat with one swipe of his claw. I thought I was going to die…" He stopped and searched their faces. "You think I'm mad, don't you?"

"No," said Tom. "We've seen some strange things, too." Castor's words had given him an idea, but he needed to discuss it with Elenna. "You must be hungry." Tom took some bread from Storm's saddlebag and handed it to Castor who attacked it ravenously, as if had not eaten for a long time.

Tom steered Elenna to a safe distance and spoke in a low whisper. "I've thought of a way to fight Krabb."

"How?" she asked. "We only just escaped last time – we're no match for the Beast on the water."

"Not *on* the water, no," said Tom. "But if we can lure Krabb to come to us, on land, perhaps we have a chance."

Elenna's eyes suddenly brightened. She glanced over at the remains of Castor's catch. "And Krabb likes to eat fish…"

"Exactly," said Tom. "But we need a line."

Elenna ran back to the remains of Castor's boat and set to work with her hunting knife, unpicking the scraps of netting. In next to no time, she'd fashioned a line that stretched out fifty paces along the beach. She used the remaining pieces of cord to tie some of the dead fish along the length of the line.

"That's incredible," said Tom. He looked over at Castor and saw that the boy had fallen asleep after his meal.

"I have an uncle who's a fisherman," Elenna said, folding her arms to admire her handiwork. "I picked up a few tricks."

Silver sniffed at one of the dead fish, then tramped away across the sand.

"Clearly not to his taste," said Tom, putting his shield on the ground. "Let's hope Krabb isn't as fussy."

He tied the little boat's anchor to the end of the line – he'd need a decent weight to carry it out to sea. Wrapping the loose end twice around his waist, Tom took hold of the anchor. He spun it around over his head, gaining speed, and then hurled it as far as he could.

The anchor carried the line far out into the deep water, where it landed with a *plop*.

With the pearl in one hand and his sword in the other, Tom stood facing the expanse of ocean, the wash of the sea lapping at his feet. He knew that his friends stood behind him, watching the sea for Krabb, just like he was. Tom frowned. Even if Krabb fell for the trap, he wasn't sure how he'd remove Velmal's enchantment – he didn't even know what the enchantment was.

All he could do was wait...

CHAPTER SEVEN

THE HUNT

Tom felt a tug on the rope.

"Elenna!" he shouted, as his hand tightened around the pearl. "Krabb's here!"

Tom ground his heels into the sand as the line tensed and pulled him forwards. He scanned the ocean where his line dipped into the water. It thrummed taut, vibrating. Tom heaved, pushing himself backwards up the beach. Elenna was there too, her hands around his waist, pulling him. It seemed to be working – they were winning their deadly tug-of-war.

Something broke the surface – but it wasn't the great, hulking body of Krabb. It was a fin, tangled up in the fishing line. Then a mouth lined with sharp teeth emerged from the waves.

A shark!

"Quick, Tom!" said Elenna. "If the shark eats all our bait, we'll have no way to lure Krabb."

Tom tried lashing the fishing line back and forth to release the creature, but he only managed to tangle the shark up even more.

"Elenna," Tom said, removing the line from around his waist. "Hold this. I'll go into the water and salvage what I can."

He sheathed his sword and took a step into the shallows, moving his amulet inside his shirt to protect it. Suddenly, a great shape rose up behind the thrashing shark. Barnacles clung to its dark shell, and eight legs rose out of the water.

Krabb!

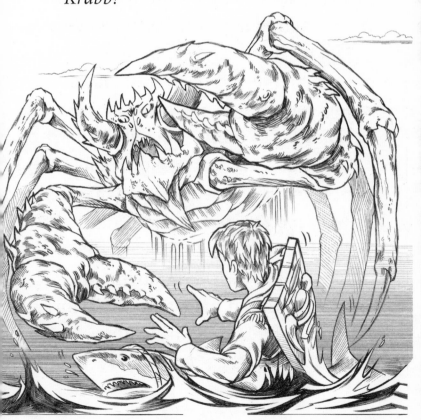

The Beast screeched as he focused on the shark. Before Tom could do anything, one of his giant pincers darted forwards, lifting the squirming shark out of the water. With a single slice, the shark's body was broken in two, both halves dropping into the sea. A fountain of blood reddened the water and the line went slack. Krabb picked up half of the shark in each pincer and pushed them into his gaping mouth.

"Come back, Tom!" shouted Elenna.

Tom shook his head. "We've got to complete this Quest. We must find a way to lure Krabb onto land."

The Beast thrashed his legs in the water and his crazed eyes rested on Tom, but he didn't attack.

"What are you thinking?" Tom asked aloud. He bent down and

picked up the loose line, hoping
that he might still be able to use it. He
quickly wrapped it around his wrist.

The Beast suddenly began to sink out
of sight once again and bubbles frothed
up around the edges of his shell.

Yank!

The line around Tom's wrist
snapped tight and he was pulled
forwards onto his knees.

"Tom!" he heard Elenna yell, and
he quickly found his feet again.
Krabb jerked once more and Tom
felt like his arm was being pulled
out of its socket. He pulled his wrist
back, trying to tow the Beast
towards the shore. Elenna rushed
to his side and gripped his free arm,
and they both pulled backwards.
Krabb tugged back again, and they
were both hauled to the ground and

dragged along on their bellies.

Tom gritted his teeth angrily as the pearl was knocked from his hand and rolled out of reach. "We're not strong enough to pull Krabb inland," he shouted to Elenna. "You have to let go!"

"But you'll be dragged into the sea," she said. "Krabb will eat you alive."

"We'll both end up in his claws if you don't let go. I need the pearl."

Elenna let go of the line and rolled away. Tom saw her scramble to her feet and run over to where the pearl rested in the sand. A wave crashed over his head and he came up spluttering. Slowly but surely he was being dragged further into the sea and closer to Krabb.

"Tom!" he heard Elenna shout. "Catch!"

He turned through the blur of water and saw his friend standing on the shore. In her hand glistened the pearl. She threw it to him, but as Tom tried to catch it, Krabb tugged him forwards once again and the pearl disappeared under the waves.

I can't lose it! It's my only chance, Tom thought. He dived beneath the surface. It was clear underwater and he could see the pearl sinking steadily. Tom kicked after it, feeling the pressure around his wrist beginning to build. Krabb was pulling at him once more.

Tom strained against the line, reaching out with his hand. His lungs felt close to bursting and bubbles rose from his mouth.

Tom's fingers closed around the pearl, just as the line around his wrist

was yanked hard. He felt himself
being dragged through the sea, as
though a powerful tide had gripped
him. The water that surrounded him
became dark and icy cold. Tom
couldn't hold his breath any longer
and opened his mouth, expecting the
sea to flood his lungs.

But it didn't. His lungs relaxed as if they were filling with air, even though there was none. His panic vanished. He breathed out. No bubbles emerged.

I can breathe! The stories about the pearl were true.

Tom twisted himself around in the water, marvelling at the pearl's powers. Carefully, he shifted the magical prize to his left hand, so he could draw his sword with his right.

Through the murky water a shadow loomed.

Krabb.

CHAPTER EIGHT

AN UNDERWATER BATTLE

Despite his size, Krabb was just as agile beneath the waves as he was above. His legs churned through the water with ease.

As Tom continued to be dragged forwards, he stared at the Beast determinedly. Somehow, he would find a way to remove Velmal's enchantment and make the Beast good again. Tom rested his blade on the taut line around his wrist. He was still about twenty boat-lengths away. *I need to get closer*, he thought.

Tom could see the hunger in Krabb's eyes as the distance between them closed. It was hard to imagine that a Beast looking so fearsome had once been a friend to Gwildor.

What's holding Krabb under Velmal's spell? Tom wondered. When Malvel had enchanted the good Beasts of Avantia, he'd done so with the help of a magic object, like a collar or a chain. Had Velmal done something similar? Tom was now ten boat-lengths from Krabb. He could see that the Beast's thick shell was covered in gouges and scrapes, but nothing unusual – just the green slime that clung to one of the Beast's pincers.

Krabb's mouth opened, ready to receive its latest victim. Inside that gaping hole, lines of small, razor-sharp teeth awaited. Tom wished he could reach his shield. Anything to protect himself from the crunching power of Krabb's jaws!

Tom knew he could leave it no longer and sliced the line around his wrist with his sword. His momentum carried him forwards, but Tom placed a foot on Krabb's thick brow and rolled over the top of the waiting jaws. He found himself with both feet planted on Krabb's shell, looking down on the Beast from above.

Krabb let out a screech of confusion, sending streams of bubbles towards the surface. His eight legs stamped up and down in the water. Tom fell to his knees.

With the pearl in one hand and his sword in the other, Tom couldn't hold on and tipped off the back of the shell, landing on top of one of Krabb's legs. He quickly gripped the Beast's limb between his knees.

Tom held on tight as the giant crab kicked out again and again, trying to dislodge him. The Beast then opened and closed his claws, but Tom was too high up for those deadly weapons to be effective.

High-pitched, angry screeches reverberated through the water, and Krabb's hungry eyes glowed furiously. Tom felt his bones jar and his teeth rattle inside his head as he continued to be tossed from side to side. It was like riding a wild horse on the plains of Avantia. *I can't hold on for much longer,* Tom thought. *I need to find the enchantment.*

Tom gave a hiss of frustration as he suddenly lost his grip and was flung away from Krabb, landing on the seabed. Instantly, one of the Beast's legs shot down towards his head and

Tom rolled away in a cloud of sand. Another leg stabbed downwards and Tom rolled again. But he was not quite quick enough. Krabb's leg caught his tunic and tore half of it away, scratching his hipbone. Tom felt anger flood his chest – moving through the water quickly was impossible.

When the next leg came towards him, Tom used the flat of his sword to bat it away. His arm was already tired – without the golden armour of his previous Quests, he had no magical strength. Tom knew he had to get above Krabb again – it was the only place he was safe.

Tom pushed off the sea floor and kicked with his legs. Krabb turned, creating a surge of current that sent Tom spinning away. He tried to swim, but was so disorientated that he didn't know which way was up.

Suddenly, everything came back into focus when a sharp pain rushed up his arm. Tom's right hand – his sword-hand – was clamped in one of the Beast's vice-like claws. Water rushed through his gritted teeth as he struggled to wriggle free.

It was no use.

Now that Krabb's got me, he's not letting go, thought Tom.

Tom was dragged towards the Beast's flexing jaws. He tried to pull his hand from the Beast's grip but it was useless – he was stuck.

Tom looked at the pearl that he

held in his left palm. *I still have one good hand*, he thought to himself. *I'll have to use it to break free.*

Taking a deep breath he released the pearl and it sank downwards. Tom knew that it was now a race against time. If he didn't escape the Beast and get back above the surface, he would suffocate beneath the sea of Gwildor.

Tom opened his throbbing right hand and let his sword drift free. It floated slowly through the water in front of his face and he snatched it up with his left hand. Tom didn't want to harm the Beast, but he was left with no choice. He saw Krabb's eyes swivel in his direction – the Beast had worked out Tom's plan.

But Krabb was not fast enough. Tom jammed his sword into the pincer holding his right hand and tried to prise it open, but it wouldn't move. His feet were almost in Krabb's mouth, and he could see the gaping, muscular chasm of the Beast's throat open, preparing to swallow him whole. Tom's chest was burning from lack of air. He swung the sword at the pincer, hacking at the tough shell. The blade lodged halfway through.

Krabb's cry echoed through the water, creating armies of bubbles that washed over Tom's body. A green cloud oozed out from the wound in the pincer and Tom was blinded. He dragged up his left arm to shield his face.

That must be Krabb's poison, he thought, remembering the green mark on Castor's back.

The pressure on his wrist suddenly

disappeared. The claw had opened. He was free!

But where was the pearl? Tom's chest felt like it was on fire, and he knew that he'd pass out before he could break the surface of the water. He needed the Mistress of the Beasts' prize if he was going to survive.

He opened his eyes slightly, and saw that the green poison had faded away. He turned in the water and locked eyes with Krabb, who was swimming straight towards him. Tom tried to hold his sword in his right hand but it still ached from being trapped in Krabb's pincer, and his whole body felt faint from lack of air.

This is it, Tom thought desperately. *The end of the Quest.*

CHAPTER NINE

THE CURSE
IS LIFTED

Tom tried to lift his sword but his
hand ached terribly. Just as he
thought Krabb's claws would cut
him in two, the Beast veered to
the side and shot past him, moving
powerfully through the water with
his giant legs.

What was Krabb doing?

Tom felt his eyes close as water

flooded his throat and the pain in his chest became unbearable.

He felt something touch his left hand. His fingers closed around it instinctively. The pain of drowning vanished like a lifting cloud. He could breathe again! Tom opened his eyes, looked down and saw he was now holding the pearl, cool and smooth.

How had that happened?

Krabb's massive form rose up in front of him, but the Beast did not attack. There was something different about him now. His eyes, which before were glowing with anger, had calmed. The pincers didn't strike out. No attack came.

A trail of green still trickled from the Beast's injured claw, and now Tom understood everything. The venom was how Velmal had controlled

Krabb! And when Tom wounded the Beast, the poison had leaked away – the evil magic going with it. It was Krabb who had helped him by retrieving the pearl from the seabed. The Beast was good once more.

Tom felt a rush of pity and also shame that he had injured such a magnificent Beast.

I'm sorry – I had no choice, he wanted to say.

Krabb extended his uninjured pincer and Tom sheathed his sword – he wouldn't need it any more. He reached out and took hold of the claw. Krabb kicked with all eight legs and they shot up towards the surface together. The water streamed past Tom and he marvelled at the Beast's power.

They broke the surface and Tom sighed with relief. It felt like he'd been underwater for days. The sun blazed down on the dappled sea, and he turned towards shore. He could see Elenna standing on the beach, looking out across the waves. Storm stood nearby, as did Silver, who appeared to be sniffing the air for Tom's scent.

Tom felt light as a leaf floating across the waves as Krabb set out in the direction of land. He could have swum himself, but his limbs ached with fatigue. When they reached the beach, Krabb lifted him gently from the water, and placed him on the shore. Tom's raised his head from the sand and he saw Elenna running along the beach, already drawing an arrow from her quiver and putting it to her bow. He realised what she was going to do.

"No, Elenna!" he croaked, his throat hoarse. "Don't!"

His friend's face creased with confusion, but she didn't loose her arrow at Krabb.

"Velmal's enchantment is broken," said Tom, struggling to his feet. "Krabb saved me, and so did this."

He held up the pearl.

Elenna lowered her bow, and ran to hug Tom.

Tom hugged his friend back. His right hand throbbed from when Krabb had grabbed him. Looking down, he could see his hand was stained with a dark green bruise. *Velmal is to blame,* he told himself. *Not the Beast.* He looked up and saw Elenna staring at Krabb uneasily.

"It's all right," said Tom. "He means no harm."

Krabb slid back into the water with barely a ripple, until only his eyes and the top of his shell broke the surface. He blew out a column of bubbles.

"He looks almost sorry," said Tom, waving to the Beast until he was out of sight.

"What happened to your hand?" asked Elenna.

Tom told Elenna about his underwater battle and how Krabb's claw had gripped him.

"The bruising is much darker than the mark on Castor's back," she said. "Your whole hand is green. Does it hurt?"

Tom flexed his fingers gingerly and gritted his teeth against the pain.

"A little," he said, trying not to worry his friend. "It must be because it's a fresh wound."

"Castor's mark is almost gone," said Elenna. "I'm sure yours will fade too, soon enough."

Tom nodded. "Of course it will," he said. "And the fishermen of Gwildor will have nothing to fear again."

The two friends walked up the beach towards Castor, who was being watched by Silver and Storm. Silver howled with joy as they drew near and Storm stamped the sand. Tom smiled. It felt good to see his companions again.

But the danger is not over yet, he reminded himself. *Velmal and Freya are still out there...*

CHAPTER TEN

THE CHOSEN ONE?

Tom was relieved to see that Castor was looking much better. The colour had returned to his cheeks and the boy was up on his feet, trying to turn over the wreck of his little boat.

"Elenna told me that you were dragged into the sea by Krabb," said the Gwildorian. "I can't believe I slept through it – I'm so sorry."

"Don't worry about it," Tom reassured him. "You were badly injured. Besides, it seems the myth about the pearl is true. It kept me safe."

"I knew it!" said Castor.

With some of his strength now returning, Tom managed to get a shoulder underneath the edge of the boy's boat, and together the three of them flipped it over. The boat was a sorry sight.

"It'll take a good carpenter to fix that," said Elenna, surveying the broken timbers.

"Then it's lucky we have several in my village! I'll bring them out to see it," Castor replied.

Tom noticed that the boy was looking at him strangely.

"You should come to meet my people," said the Gwildorian. "They all know the prophecy; now they'll see that it's true…"

But it can't be about me, thought Tom. *I'm not a son of Gwildor.*

The mystical words turned over and over in his head. He longed to ask Castor more – where did the prophecy start? Who first issued it?

Tom shook his head. Every kingdom had its own stories, legends that were passed down from generation to

113

generation. It was foolish to believe them all. Aduro had sent him here for a reason. He had to concentrate on the Quests ahead. Gwildor was in danger until the five remaining Beasts were freed. And if Gwildor was in peril, Avantia would surely be next.

Tom made up his mind. "I'm sorry," he told Castor, "but our path lies...elsewhere."

Elenna seemed about to say something, but stopped when she saw Tom's face. She understood that they couldn't rest until the Beast Quest was completed.

"If you insist," said Castor. "But I must be getting back. My parents will be worried about me. Goodness knows what I'll tell them – a giant crab, the pearl of Gwildor...they'll never believe me!"

Tom and Elenna laughed.

"Goodbye, then," said the Gwildorian boy. "And thank you for everything."

"Goodbye," Tom said.

"Take care," said Elenna. Silver howled farewell, too.

Tom watched Castor run off along the beach and disappear into the trees. He turned to Storm and patted his flank. "Are you ready for more adventures, boy?"

"He's ready," said a voice, "but are you?"

Tom turned to see Aduro and Taladon standing side-by-side on the beach. For a moment he thought they were really with him in Gwildor, but their feet made no marks in the sand – they were apparitions.

"You have triumphed, Tom," said Aduro, "and Krabb is free again. But I must warn you, even more dangerous challenges lie ahead."

"We will not be able to visit often," said Taladon. "As you move deeper into Gwildor, Velmal's magic will grow stronger and Aduro's will

become weaker. You will have to rely on your own resources then."

"Don't worry, Father," Tom said. "I'll be prepared to face Velmal. And Freya will be, too."

Taladon's face paled. Aduro lowered his eyes.

"What's the matter?" Elenna asked.

"You have seen the Mistress of the Beasts?" Taladon asked. "Velmal showed her to you?"

"He did," said Tom, remembering Freya's cruel laughter.

Taladon turned to Aduro and spoke in quiet, urgent tones. Tom strained to hear, but the only words he could make out were "even worse than we thought".

The wizard nodded gravely, and addressed Tom and Elenna. "Always be on your guard, champions of

Avantia. And remember, though the people of Gwildor are good, darkness and evil lurk in the shadows."

"Wait… Why are things worse than you thought?" asked Tom.

But the two apparitions began to fade. Tom didn't know if they'd heard his question or not, and in a moment they were gone completely.

Dusk had settled on Gwildor and the moon began to rise. Tom mounted Storm then helped Elenna up behind him.

"I think Aduro is keeping something from us," he said to his friend.

"If we stick together, we'll be fine," she replied.

Questions swirled in Tom's mind. Five Beasts awaited inland – five innocents imprisoned by Velmal.

Tom took the reins in his hands.

"Ready?" he asked.

Elenna's hands gripped his waist. "Absolutely. I'm always ready to begin a new Quest!"

Tom spurred Storm on and they galloped up the beach towards the trees. Silver raced beside them.

As they entered the forest again, Tom suspected there might be more surprises to come. But Elenna was right – with his three companions by his side, no Beast Quest was too great.

Here's a sneak preview of Tom's
next exciting adventure!

Meet

HAWKITE
ARROW OF
THE AIR

Only Tom can free the Beasts from
Velmal's wicked enchantment...

PROLOGUE

The field lay devastated. The crops were
flattened to the ground, and good for nothing.
Harvin and his father walked through the
broken wheat stalks, gazing at the remains
of the harvest.

"I can't believe it," Harvin's father groaned.
"Another ruined crop."

It was too much. They couldn't go on like
this. Harvin knew his father had nothing left to
sell. Their barn was empty, their livestock long
gone. Everywhere in Gwildor, people were
desperate for food. And now this...

Harvin's stomach growled hungrily. "What
will we eat tonight?" he asked.

His father shook his head. "I don't know,"
he said. "These storms... They come from
nowhere and ruin everything."

He fell silent and Harvin knew that his
father was thinking of how they had so nearly
lost their farmhouse in the night. The wind
had torn at the roof shingles and battered the
windows until the panes of glass had shattered.

The air suddenly grew cold. A shadow fell

across the ruined field, passing over Harvin and his father. They looked up and fell to their knees in terror. Something was flying overhead. Even though it was high in the sky, its vast wings cast a shadow that ran from one end of the field to the other. It looked like a hawk. But it couldn't be – it was too big, and its bald head was like that of a vulture.

The Beast screamed in fury. Harvin flinched as it swooped downwards. Its gigantic shadow grew closer. Everything turned black as it plummeted towards them.

Now they could see its cruel talons, razor-sharp, angled towards them. A vile stench, like dead flesh, made Harvin gag and cover his nose. The Beast continued to swoop down, cutting through the air like a black arrow. Harvin could see its evil eyes, glinting red. Something was glowing on the underside of one wing – green feathers, strange and out of place on the immense fiery-coloured bird.

"We're going to die!" whispered Harvin. He grasped his father's hand and trembled with terror.

The Beast beat its mighty wings and the wind

struck them like a sledgehammer. Trees on the edges of the field crashed to the ground, splintering in the force of the gale. The last crops were torn up by their roots and flung into the air. Harvin managed to grab onto a fence post. He clung to it as the wind tried to rip the clothes off his back. He could feel his father's grip on his other hand loosening as the wind tugged at him. It was no good. His father couldn't hold on.

**Follow this Quest to the end in
HAWKITE ARROW OF THE AIR.**

Win an exclusive
Beast Quest T-shirt and goody bag!

In every Beast Quest book the Beast Quest logo is hidden in one of the pictures. Find the logos in books 25 to 30 and make a note of which pages they appear on. Write the six page numbers on a postcard and send it in to us. Each month we will draw one winner to receive a Beast Quest T-shirt and goody bag.

THE BEAST QUEST COMPETITION:
THE SHADE OF DEATH

Orchard Books
338 Euston Road, London NW1 3BH

Australian readers should email:
childrens.books@hachette.com.au

New Zealand readers should write to:
Beast Quest Competition
4 Whetu Place, Mairangi Bay, Auckland, NZ
or email: childrensbooks@hachette.co.nz

Only one entry per child.
Final draw: 29 October 2010

You can also enter this competition
via the Beast Quest website: www.beastquest.co.uk

Join the Quest,
Join the Tribe

www.beastquest.co.uk

Have you checked out the all-new Beast Quest website?
It's the place to go for games, downloads, activities,
sneak previews and lots of fun!

You can read all about your favourite Beasts, download
free screensavers and desktop wallpapers for your
computer, and even challenge your friends
to a Beast Tournament.

Sign up to the newsletter at www.beastquest.co.uk
to receive exclusive extra content and the opportunity
to enter special members-only competitions. We'll send
you up-to-date info on all the Beast Quest books,
including the next exciting series which features
six brand-new Beasts!

Series 5
BEAST QUEST

Tom must travel to Gwildor, Avantia's twin kingdom, to free six new Beasts from an evil enchantment...

978 1 40830 437 2

978 1 40830 438 9

978 1 40830 439 6

978 1 40830 440 2

978 1 40830 441 9

978 1 40830 442 6

978 1 40830 436 5

Can Tom rescue the precious Cup of Life from a deadly two-headed demon?

Series 6: WORLD OF CHAOS
COMING SOON!

978 1 40830 723 6

978 1 40830 724 3

978 1 40830 725 0

978 1 40830 726 7

978 1 40830 727 4

978 1 40830 728 1

978 1 40830 735 9

Does Tom have the strength to triumph over cunning Creta?